A Gift of the Sea

Tristan Gray

ISBN: 978-1-8384854-4-3

ACKNOWLEDGMENTS

With each entry I publish in this series I become more confident and secure in my process, and that all comes down to having the same team with me every step of the way.

There are few things that can compete for a sense of happiness and belonging than a partner who loves and supports you through your journey. Jude has been there for me over the past years, and its with that support I do my best as a writer.

To my family, who continue to be a constant inspiration and encouragement even whilst we're trapped hundreds of miles away from one another, I hope to see you all this year, at last!

Thank again to Gillian Hamnett from Dark Sky Pages for her work bringing the Scots leid to life in these pages with Annis. Including the language in my work is a vital part of giving back to the place and culture that inspires me, and Gillian ensures those words are given the attention they deserve.

Thank you to Margaret Kingsbury, editor for Salt & Sage Books, for her work on the developmental edit. Her constructive and encouraging feedback makes these stories what they are, every time.

Thanks to Matthew King who yet again took the hit of being the first friend to read this one and check it for all the little slip ups and errors than can make it into the final edit. Every find is one less to frustrate a reader diving into self-published work!

Content warning for off-page rape and abduction.

A GIFT OF THE SEA

The trail down into Tur Pailt was slick with rain, every flash of lightning lighting up the water cascading off the rocks.

Fiadh and Annis had long since dismounted and guided their steeds down the path with care, mindful of the yawning gap beside them and the roar of waves crashing against the base of the cliffs.

"Whit brings us tae this forsaken steid, Fiadh?"

"A job, Annis. It's always a job. A man who's lost a brother sent me a letter in the hopes a Crow might find him, even though an Rìgh, as usual, could not."

"An Rìgh?" Annis replied, his southern accent mangling the words in her tongue, "that's the Laird Pailt?"

"The very same. I'll put down five pieces that the Laird didn't shift from his tower an inch for the effort," the slick rocks shifted beneath Fiadh's feet and she swore as she regained her footing.

"Ye ken the man?"

"I know him. He was a feared man once, Rìgh Tuath,

laird of lairds over these waters, with the rulers of every isle as far as you could see paying homage to him. Now every petty merchant in this crumbling backwater sees themselves as the true power of these seas." Fiadh had to shout over the din.

A crack of lightning and an immediate rumble answering it helped emphasise her words.

Tur Pailt was a shambling place, sheltered within a cup carved into the cliffs, buildings scattered about the cove as if they had been thrown up against it by the waves. A lone tower struck out from the shore, the fire burning at its peak shining a solitary light beneath the tumultuous sky, bright enough that Fiadh could see it even as the howling winds burned her eyes.

They ventured down the twisting path, hugging close to its granite sides and past shutters sealed tight against the weather. The Rìgh's stronghold overshadowed them, its broad stone bulk standing out against the wood and slate of the buildings about it.

The home the letter had directed them to closely matched the description they had been given. It sat beneath the empty arms of a birch; its green painted door illuminated by the flashes of lightning.

Fiadh gave a nod and Annis approached it, giving the door several firm knocks. The roar of the sea and storm didn't hide the squeal of furniture being moved within, as if the door had been blocked, before the door whipped open in the face of the wind. Beyond the door a blurry silhouette of a figure within waved them in.

Their host struggled to push the door back and Annis was forced to lend an arm to hold it in place as he pushed drawers against it to hold it shut.

The lock bar that might have held the door had been

torn free, the bent remnants propped up nearby.

"The Crow?" he said between heavy breaths.

"One of them, yes," Fiadh replied, perching on the rough-hewn table set across the far side of the fire pit. Despite the wind they had let in the pit still smouldered, the remains filling the chamber with much needed warmth and an unfortunate stench of well-cooked fish that must have preceded their arrival. She peered through the wafting smoke between them and examined the man before her. He was small, almost gaunt, eyes sunken into dark sockets.

There was an awkward silence as the man turned on crutches seemingly cobbled-together from leftovers from a boat's oar and tiller but etched with delicate swirling carvings and patterns. He learned upon them on the one leg not missing from the knee down and glanced back and forth between the visitor who had just made herself at home at his table to her companion who stood cross-armed at his own door.

"Erm, I am Eadan, you must have received my notice? My brother, Rònan, has been lost. An Rìgh has not sought to find him, and I am no seafarer myself." The man's hands clasped one another as he shifted his weight uncomfortably over his crutch.

Annis, as was his role, did a stellar job of looking stern and imposing even as the man continued to mutter in Cànan, a tongue her companion could barely grasp a single word of. In this company, however, the act was maybe a little bit too much.

"Lost?" Fiadh asked, finally relaxing her legs by hoisting herself up to perch on the edge of a chest leaning against the far wall.

"My brother was lost to the sea, I fear."

This was new. People didn't reach out to a Crow to fish for corpses, let alone for a reward promising not just coin, but silver. This must have been a brotherly bond like no other. His name would mean little, she thought, a dead man's name would not identify him.

The man noted her quizzical look and hurried to clarify what he meant. "He was in search of an item of great power, meant to tie the very soul of the sea to the bearer's will. I believe he was convinced that it lay not far from these very shores."

"So, are we looking for the item, or your brother?" Fiadh said, running his description through her mind. There were tales aplenty of trinkets and relics that were meant to seize control of the untameable seas, but none for generations more substantial than a song or a con. This was likely no different.

Their host looked genuinely astonished by the question, and the look seemed genuine, as if any other motive other than finding his brother had not even crossed his mind.

"My… my brother, of course," he stammered. "I don't have any need for whatever power he went searching for. I told him he was a fool to go searching for it, that nothing could truly win him what he seeks. But he went anyway, without me or my aid, and now he is lost."

Guilt, then. There were few stronger forces more able to separate a man from his silver.

"And what did he truly seek, your brother?" she asked, nodding to Annis that he could relax. There was no threat here.

"A woman, of course. Whatever else would that disaster of a man be chasing out into the raging seas?"

Eadan sighed, shuffling over to the chair Fiadh had left nearby and dropping heavily into it, his crutch left leaning against the table.

"A woman… never just any woman… the woman," Eadan continued with some bitterness, the words coming slowly, as if he had to drag them out from where he'd have preferred to leave them, discarded. "The one he raved on about any chance he had, the one already in the arms of the most powerful man of Tur Pailt, whose beautiful ethereal eyes he had met between market stalls, whose fleeting glances and moments he valued before all else. Before even his own life, he claimed."

"For those eyes he has gone out to seas off the Àirde Sgreamhail, declaring he'd return with the sea itself as his servant to whisk her away, to carry her to his new kingdom of the waves."

Fiadh's eyebrows went up at that, frowning in thought. Those were mighty grand words even for a young man newly besotted, and at no minor risk either. The screaming cliffs were not known for their hospitality, nor were the tales of men snatched below the waves at their feet an idle threat. When Annis raised his own eyebrows in response, she translated into Àrdish briefly. "Lad with eyes on a lass went to sea for something shiny to win her with."

Annis nodded matter-of-factly to that. It wasn't the most original of stories.

"So, you're offering us enough to buy yourself a fèinne just to find your fool of a brother and return him?" she asked, pandering to his desire to see his brother alive once more. Truly, this long lost at sea, long enough to seek aid, be denied it, and seek out a Crow instead, his remains were either washed upon some rock or he had long sailed for another shore. She cast her eyes around the room as the man gathered his own thoughts. It was a simple place of no more than a handful of chambers. A place of some comfort, true, built sturdy against the seasons and with space aplenty, but not burnished with a wealth that suggested there was much to be thrown into the grave of a man possibly lying fifty feet beneath the waves.

"How come you by these riches?" she asked, peering into the shadows of the room.

"What does it matter? I've invited you, armed, into my home, shown you where I store my coin, is not a little trust to be reciprocated?"

"Sure, and since we didn't barge in here, kill you, and steal your coin," Fiadh's voice lowered. "Maybe you could sate my curiosity before I set out into these fearful seas to look for your brother in a nest of monsters."

He gulped at that. "I'm a carpenter, I make designs and figurines for wealthy patrons. No one else does, this side of the mountains, so they fetch a fair price."

She cocked an eyebrow. "No one else carves people from wood?"

"No one like me," he replied, with some confidence coming back into his voice.

There was a silence for a moment as Fiadh looked across the chamber again, weighing up the potential that there was something more to this. This would not have been the first time an offer of coin beyond their usual taking turned out to be some kind of trap, or a con spun to make a display of a changeling drawn into the wheelings and dealings of spiteful men.

He broke the silence. They often did, eventually, unnerved by silver-eyed fey guests and the implacable silence of Annis.

"You're not the first to come by, on seeing my notice," he said, his eyes no longer meeting hers.

Here we are, she thought, and more easily than she had anticipated.

A nervous glance from him in her direction caught her curious gaze, prompting him on. "Hooded men, Crow, red robes from the south, asking if one all in black with silvered eyes had passed by since my notice went out. They didn't speak Cànan so well and muttered to one another in the tongue of your companion, furtive like, as if they were expecting you to leap upon them from the shadows at any moment."

Now this was a tale worth the journey. Fiadh immensely enjoyed hearing how the tale of Ghav Rhien had been spun in the months since she had left that haunted isle.

"They were searching for you, or any word of your passing," Eadan continued. "That blade you carry at your shoulder; I recognise it from their description. Caerdrich, they called it. They call you the blood weaver." He shuddered; his eyes cast to the floor. "They say you have a spindle to draw out the life of innocent men, and that you bathe in it to stay young."

Fiadh barked out a laugh at that, both Annis and Eadan jumping at the sudden sound as she clapped her hands together.

"A bath!" she shouted with open glee. "Oh, I would absolutely murder someone for a bath!"

There was no laugh from the pale faced Eadan, and Annis looked, not for the first time, as if she had finally lost her mind.

"You have won me over, Eadan," she continued "it

takes nerve to invite a 'blood weaver' into your home and offer them gold, all to win back a brother lost at sea. I appreciate nerve, and I'll take your coin for the pleasure."

"You… you want to help me more knowing that the Order are searching for you here?" Eadan looked more nervous than he had done since they'd entered. His free hand gripped fast around a pendant hanging from his neck.

"I want to help you more now that I know you're not hiding anything from me. Who knows, maybe your brother is still lives out there on the seas and your faith in his survival might yet be repaid." Fiadh turned to Annis and broke the news that they'd be setting out on the water soon, to find their horses and packs somewhere safe to shelter. His expression matched the weather they were due to head out in, but with a nod and a final puzzled look at the woodcarver he let himself out.

"So, any more detail on where he might be? And what I might return should he be lost, to prove his passing to you?" she said, standing and wandering around the small abode, looking for evidence of the man's artistic talent.

"He… he said he had to search the seas off the cliffs. There's a wreck out there, impaled on rocks a few hundred yards from the shore." He paused for a moment, as if asking for her permission to continue. "It's been there since before I was born. They say the Daoine Sìth sailed to an ancient home beyond the waves upon it, and their magics still bind it from decay to this day. He will have had his ring upon him." He brought forward his hand and she turned to look upon it, a roughly hewn iron ring sat around his middle finger, two fish carved into its surface. "We have worn them ever since we were children, as a mark of our love for one another. He'll be wearing it out there, somewhere."

Having memorised the ring's design, she continued the search for his work and finally found one, a small carving no larger than her hand of a horse with the hindquarters replaced with the tail of a fish. It stood out from its surroundings; the wood delicately carved and smooth enough to reflect the glow of the embers even as it rested on a table-top hewn so roughly as to risk splinters. It was exquisite! The detail of every hair of its mane picked out, every scale of its tail. She had never seen anything quite like it.

A man of such talent, bound to one who would throw it all away on a folktale. The heart was so often loyal beyond the wisdom that might guide us, she thought.

"The cliffs? I know where they are. I have just one thing to ask of you before I depart," she said, gently returning the figure to its place upon the window ledge.

"What's that?" he replied, a slight tremor to his voice.

"Is there a chance you have any wax?"

***

"Found a place for the horses?" she shouted, pulling the hood of her cloak down hard against the wind.

"Did ah say ah hadnae?" came the reply, Annis not bothering to turn as he picked his way through the shore's rocks and pebbles.

"Well, no, but…"

"Weel then, there's yer answer."

Annis didn't speak much at the best of times, but he'd been particularly quiet today, ever since they'd left the carpenter's home.

"You need to smile when death comes knocking, Annis," she yelled over to him, sliding away down towards the water. "It'll come often enough. If you don't smile when you can you'll end up never smiling at all. If the Ríagan wills it, we'll pass."

"Is this bloody rain the Ríagan's wull as weel, then?" he said, turning towards her as she slipped away further towards the shoreline, the water running through the close shorn stubble of his scalp and past eyes squinted against it.

"The Ríagan hasn't spoken to me since I was a child. I haven't heard her voice since the fall of the Tur," she shouted up towards him, the grind of wet pebbles shifting under her feet cloaking her words. "I have heard many other voices in the dark, but never hers," she continued, as much to herself as to her companion. "I hope, once those responsible for the death of her heralds have been reacquainted with Caerdrich, I might hear her voice again."

There, ahead of them, was what they had been searching for, winding their way from cove to cove between the cliffs. The rowboat had been dragged up past the seaweed that marked the high-tide line, lobster pots and nets crowded into one end of it.

"I told you we'd find one!" Fiadh said.

"Aye, ye did." he replied, joining her, and looking over the small craft, barely large enough for a single seat between the oars.

"But what if you fall in?" he asked, sceptical eyes taking in the waves lapping at the shore.

Fiadh stood up from where she had been checking its underside for any leaks or cracks. "Feel my hand," she said, holding her bare fingers out towards him.

He looked a little taken aback at the request. "Go on, hold it."

His lip twisted slightly as he held out a hand and gently wrapped his fingers around hers. He hid it well, but she felt the muscles of his arm tense at the sensation, the warmth of his skin vanishing into the cold depths of her own.

"Does that feel like flesh like your own, Annis, that should fear the creeping cold of the sea?"

"No, it feels like a bluidy corpse."

She wasn't expecting that, and his words stung more than she was prepared for. She brought her fingers free of his loose grip and hid them within her cloak once more.

"A corpse is what I might well have been when I fell from the Tur, Annis. I gave away something of myself to walk on land again. The sea didn't claim me then, I have faith it will not do so now."

Annis' brows were knotted with concern as he looked sceptically towards the rowboat and the sea beyond, then up to the cliffs that loomed above in the moonlight and that lone rock framed upon the horizon.

Fiadh stood with him in silence a moment. The sounds washed over them, the rhythmic crash and roll of the waves, the faint ringing of water striking the pebbles and running between them, and the far-off voices of those who watched from the cliffs that her ears could hear but his could not. The voices reminded her of a rhyme from long ago, when she had listened to these same sounds from far above these dark waters.

"Don't worry for me, Annis, I have been into these waters plenty of times before. Besides, I have you completing a vital task, here to guide me back to the shore," she said as she unshouldered her sack and knelt to move through its contents, pulling free a lantern encased on three sides with metal and on the fourth in coloured glass. "The cliffs ahead earned their name in our tongue from horrors far more deadly than cold water and sharpened rocks."

"Now," she said, standing and holding the lantern towards him. "I need you to ensure this is lit and remains lit until I return. The rain will cloak the rocks so I cannot see the route back, and I will not be able to hear your voice."

Annis took the lantern from her hand, letting it hang as she took up flint and steel and began to light sparks within its chamber. As it caught the oil-soaked wick and she closed the glass window at its front, she reached back down and pulled out the wax Eadan had spared her.

"Any questions before I head out?"

Annis screwed up his nose and looked back out at the water through the rain dripping from his eyelashes. "Nah, ah'm guid. Ah'll staun an' git drookit, an' point the licht at the sea. Ah'll wait fur ye tae row back wi' a deid yin, then wander back an' git oor reward."

Fiadh nodded as she massaged the wax between her fingers, struggling to soften it against the cold.

She kept kneading them in one hand as she set about unloading the nets and pots from the boat, tossing the last of it aside just as Annis put one foot against the hull and gave it a shove towards the waterline.

The sodden pebbles underfoot crunched and

squealed as she put a shoulder against the wood and gave it another shove out onto the water, her own boots holding back the water but not the chill that pricked at her calves as she strode into the lapping waves.

Hopping aboard she made herself at home. Two oars were fixed in rowlocks on either side and a handy bench sat between them for the work ahead. She settled in, thumbs pushing the wax deep into her ears. Another shove from Annis had the boat on its way out, and she gave his grim furrowed brows a final wave as she took up the oars, glancing back from the light into the darkness stretching out behind her.

Immediately, with her ears clogged against the din of the storm, she could hear her heart throbbing, the sudden bellowing rush of her own breath as she wrenched the oars into place and began to row herself out to sea. The sounds came with every pull she took a breath and with every pounding second she glanced over her shoulders at the stretch of waves that tossed her craft like a plaything rolling in her palm.

She could see the cliffs begin to rise from the pebbled beach, their pitch-black crags framed against the dull grey of the clouds beyond, shimmering under the rain's tumult.

In time they made themselves known, moving across the rocks at the base of the cliffs, their scales flashing back the grey of the skies and the light that bounded upon the waves. Fiadh could see their mouths open, calling to her as her vessel touched each crest before spilling down the other side once more.

The merrow of the Àirde Sgreamhail were coming for her, their song sounding across the waters, beckoning her to join them in the depths. She knew what songs they sang; she had heard them before as an older Crow held her shoulder tight, looking out and listening from a distance. She knew their song's pull, the way it had pricked and tugged at her mind, drawing her to join them, to plunge into the depths and swim with their melody.

To die there, like so many others tempted to their end.

They knew their song went unheard, their scales flashing as they ducked in and out of view between the waves, spiralling ever nearer to her craft. She fixed her eyes ahead, back towards that lonely golden light on the shore, where Annis awaited her return. She had heard about their beautiful faces, more beautiful than any she could ever know, their perfect features appearing between beckoning fingers to coax you into their reach so you might never escape their song again.

The mighty pinnacle of rock that jutted from the centre of the bay was beginning to loom ever larger now, its black expanse beginning to block the way onward. The effort to steer the boat began to gnaw at her back and shoulders, her neck aching as she struggled to drag the boat back on course as waves knocked it this way and that, her forearms burning even as she flexed and rolled her fingers against the wood to rest her grip with each pull.

She caught them in the corners of her vision, their scales breaching the water one by one, fins briefly flashing and letting gentle sprays fly free to challenge the rain. They were circling, drawing in like a net enclosing her pitiful craft knocked about by the shifting waves.

The great rock was not alone above the waves, its passenger growing clearer with every stroke of the oar and every glance over her shoulder. A ship rose from the sea, impaled on that pyramid of stone, its bow embracing it with shattered timbers. Its hull seemed to glimmer as the beams of moonlight struck it, the green that wrapped the woodwork shining like emeralds.

It was enormous, like no ship she had ever laid eyes on before. Greater than the trade ships the Àrdish sailed from southern shores weighed down with cargo, greater than the largest longships filled with horses and powered by a score of oars the Sjøfolk sailed from their far-off home.

The rowboat shuddered as it ran aground on barnacled rocks, jerking Fiadh forwards and onto her feet as she scrambled to keep hold of the oars. She pulled them in, running them under the seats at its rear and hopping onto the rocks herself, giving it a final haul up and out of the water. Looking back over the water she saw nothing but waves, no sign of the Merrow, as if rock itself had dismissed them back to the black cliffs circling the bay.

It was not only the wreck of the ship itself that had shone that green hue. Seaweed clung to it, hanging in sheets from the wood and pouring out onto the rock as if the two had long become one, looming together over the sea. Fiadh ran her fingers over the wood, its surface slick with water and algae. Sharp barnacles and limpets wreathed the lowest reaches, blurring the line between wood and rock.

She planted a foot into the crevice the ship's bow was embedded into and reached up to the woodwork, working her fingers into the carvings and giving them a tug to secure her hold. She pulled herself from the rock and up to the side of the hull, her free foot gaining purchase against the rough shells on the rock.

The climb was slow and difficult, the handholds slippery and her grip tired from the rowing. But the rain was easing, and her silvered eyes found cracks and shadows in the green glow of the woodwork, openings for her fingers to grip and boots to push from.

A final shove took her over a gunwale and onto the deck, the entire surface wreathed in thick seaweed, twisting in green, red, and brown patterns. Below her the sea's surface writhed, the waves writhed into whirlpools and eddies as it ran around the broken remnants of the mast.

There, held above the water's surface by a stand that extended into the cruel grasp of eagle's talons, was a horn bound in bronze and leather as long as her forearm.

Fiadh stepped towards the mast, gradually sliding her boots through the weeds with her hands spread out for balance. Her eyes lit upon the engravings on the horn's surface, of bare-skinned men with circular shields and long spears challenging one another, of horses formed from the froth of waves, of a script that flowed in both sharp edges and curves in an ancient tongue.

As she neared it, she felt the strength that dwelled within, the air that shimmered before its mouth, parting the rain before it. The scripts on its surface glowed with the faintest of lights, as if dulled by the passage of aeons.

She reached towards it and her fingers felt the prick of the magics that filled the space around it. Fiadh was not alone feeling its power; Caerdrich felt it too. The rain about her sharpened as the tips of every drop froze with the blade's awakening, biting at her cheeks. The blade yearned for the magic, they called to it, bidding her to draw nearer. She shook away their demands. Not yet, not so hastily.

So, this was the subject of the brother's journey. An object of great power left behind by the Daoine Sìth before they vanished below the earth and into the world beyond our own, a legend that had proved truer than most. One whose command could not only win the love of the one he sought, but also compel others to clear his path to her. Had he made it this far? Braved the waters he'd have known far better than she, withstood the call of the merrow and looked upon this great relic as she did now?

He could not have been the first to be drawn to this place, to this emerald ship so close to the shore. But still the horn sat, undisturbed upon its stand. Where had he gone?

As if to answer her thoughts, the wood beneath her feet shifted and quaked, the entire bulk of the ship shuddering as if someone had grabbed its bow and tugged it towards the sea's surface.

Fiadh turned and steadied her stance, twisting her heels into the deck to steady herself in a wide fighter's stance.

She could see it through the gloom and tilt of rain, the sheen of light scattering over shifting scales, a great body slick with the downpour and sea spray, is bulk running over the woodwork of the figurehead, gripping it tight.

From the scales emerged flesh and from that flesh the torso of a woman towering above the ship, arms held wide, hair dark as night, spilling over her form from a frost-white brow.

The ceasg smiled, her teeth gleaming the rainbow of

pearls and glinting with the sharpness of blades.

"We meet again, Caerdrich!" Her voice sprung across the air and into the back of Fiadh's head, scraping beneath the drumbeat of her heart and the thunder of her breath. The wax in her ears did nothing to diminish the sound. "How long has it been since I raised you up from these depths? One thousand moons? Two?" The blade did not answer, but their readiness remained, their call to her to turn back and seize the horn even beneath the gaze of a new, monstrous, companion.

The skin of the ceasg shone with the oil of a creature from the depths, her eyes bright in the darkness like stars grasped from the sky and placed into the sockets of a skull that could be seen beneath translucent skin.

"Now you bring me a new plaything, blade, how generous." The muscles of her tail bunched beneath those shining scales, flashing their greys and whites beneath the light of the moon that had begun to peek from behind the rain clouds above. They coiled around the figurehead tight, threatening to snap it from its perch and carry it into the currents below.

"It was… it was not the blade that brought me," Fiadh said, her voice catching in her throat as she gazed up at the towering creature framed by the emerging moon. "I brought myself."

The blade did not share its desires so directly as that, not in the years since it had spoken to her upon the Tur. Their bargain did not stretch so far as such guidance, it seemed. Nor now did it deem to speak, its frozen touch no longer gripping the spray nor its thoughts revealing their connections to this master of the depths.

The ceasg leant forward from her perch, her hair spilling downwards but drifting in the air like fronds of weeds suspended in the water.

"I am sure you believe you did," the ceasg's words trailed, as if every statement were a suggestion tugging at her like the song of the Merrow beneath the waves. "I know what you are, little bird, I know you fluttered down from your nest upon the Tur. I know your wings were clipped and singed by the Raven's fiery breath. I know you are not strong enough to have come this far alone."

The words sliced through Fiadh and left her weak at the knees, the blood running from her face.

"I have come here in search of another, great one," Fiadh said, her voice weaker than she had intended, barely above a whisper. "A man's brother came here in search of the horn..."

"Your words bore me, little bird," the voice sprang back and cut off her words. "I have become accustomed to the verse of the filí who have come to me in search of wisdom and tales, whose tongues dance on the wind and woo me with their weaving speech. Why do you not sing for me, small one?"

Fiadh was frozen, for the first time feeling the cold of her rain-soaked leathers seeping through to her skin, the icy bite of Caerdrich at her back scraping at her bones. The first words of songs began to flash in her mind.

But it was not a song that finally emerged from her lips to this ancient survivor of a time long vanished, but that rhyme she had learned from the shores, held by the shoulder by her teacher, that proud warrior of the Sciathán Dubh.

"The wings that rise from Tur Eumor,

That sweep aloft and over shore,
To keep their watch out to the sea,
Here, hear how the Crow came to be."

The ceasg withdrew up towards her figurehead, a smile dancing upon her lips. "The little bird speaks but will not sing. No tunes to carry your spirit away on the winds, to prevent me from casting your body to my children with the tide."

"You lifted the blade from the sea," Fiadh replied, placing a hand on Caerdrich's hilt. "You know their power. You know that should I have come here to take from you what I had not earned, I would have come with their blade in my hand, not sheathed upon my back." Her voice broke free of its whisper so that she was now shouting above the crashing waves, her hand releasing the sword's hilt and returning to her side. "I come only seeking what was lost by another, so that I may return it to their hand."

"You come seeking the man who claimed what was lost by the sea so that he might call it his own," the voice answered, swirling in her mind. "Do you come to make that claim as well? Do you come seeking to deceive the sea, to steal what is not yours?"

Fiadh's mind raced. She knew this creature could snuff her before she could draw Caerdrich from their sheath. Their presence at her back had bought her time, for now, but only for as long as the ceasg continued to find her more interesting than tiresome.

The horn was here. So, what had Eadan claimed? What had he sought to take which the sea had already lost? That he had sought, what the horn was only a tool to win… the girl at the market! Perhaps it was not something the sea had lost, but someone.

"That which you have lost, she still lives in Tur Pailt," she said, trying as hard as she could not to let the uncertainty she felt seep into her voice.

"I know where she is, little bird, I feel her when she comes to the shore and looks out upon the waves that should be hers by right. She was taken from the waves, stolen." Those pearly teeth shone as that final word twisted and sank in her mind, bleeding darkness. "Your questing boy sought the horn to claim her as his own. He promised her return, but the sea knew his lie, so the sea claimed his life as payment. He may try to claim her once more from the beyond, if he is so convinced of their destiny to be together."

The ceasg's expression was that of gleeful contempt, a smile more menacing even than those shining eyes peering from dark depths.

The boy had come here looking for something to take the woman, Fiadh realised, not to win her. She was of the sea and somehow trapped on the land, held there in a way not even the ceasg could release her from.

She had heard of this before. Some tales spoke of people managing to identify and capture those of the sea, taking something from them that prevented them from returning to the waters. Something they could not take back, something that had to be returned to them willingly by those who held it.

"His ship is not here, is it?" she asked, hoping to buy herself time to identify a way out, and a bargain that could be struck.

"Here? Hah!" the ceasg's laughter was cruel and spiteful. "Half a man and barely half a sailor. His pitiful craft is long shattered and scattered on the waves."

"Now this, this craft you stand upon, this is a ship!" For all the ceasg claimed to love the tales of the filí, it was clear she was keener still to have an audience to tell her own.

"I have ruled over this ship for generations before he so much as danced along the sand for the first time," she continued, casting her arms wide as if she still saw it afloat rather than ground against the rock. "The navigator of this vessel was a scholar, an adventurer, a name that will ring through the ages as a titan of his day."

She was seized by her own thoughts now, paying Fiadh little mind. "Oh, for a man like him again, sailing on the waves with gods at his shoulder, bringing me tales of seas which do not move with the tides, of oceans swum by creatures I may never witness with mine own eyes."

"Instead, I face nothing but greed and lies." The ceasg flung an arm out as if to act out her throwing the sailor into the waves. "If he had truly loved her, he would have gifted her the sea. He would have returned her skin to her, freed her to return to the home that was taken from her. But no, he held only lust and the need to possess her. His greed was to take what had not been given. He drowned in that greed, but even as it filled his lungs, he screamed for what he wanted for himself and had not a moment of doubt that he she was owed to him."

Her skin? Fiadh thought, a selkie, perhaps, beings who take the shape of seals in the waters and humans upon the land - who might be trapped upon the land should their fur be stolen from them after they had shed it upon the shore.

"I would ask for one thing alone," Fiadh said, fixing her eyes on the ceasg's own even as her heart raced at the very idea of asking for more. "I would ask for something to take home to the man's brother, to remember him by. As despicable as his brother was, he is alone, now, and even should he be joined by another to share his life with, it may calm his heart to hold a reminder of what he had, and which is now lost."

It was frighteningly still as she looked deep into those pin drops of stars shining from within the ceasg's eyes. There was no expression in them, no emotion to give away her intent.

"What, pray, would you ask for by which this pitiful excuse for a man might yet be remembered upon the land?"

"I come only for the ring he bore upon his finger so that I may prove his passing to those on the shore," Fiadh replied, flexing her fingers to restore blood to their tips. "A ring bearing the mark of his brother, of two fish intertwined, so that he may be laid to rest in the memories of his loved ones."

"The ring, that is all," she continued. "The one I describe to you. It was the mark of his brother, who, despite himself, held his brother dearly. If I could return it, I could set his mind at rest, if little else."

"Very well," the ceasg conceded, "you will have your band, it is of no consequence to the sea. But he will remain taken, to feed the denizens of the waters he sought to steal from."

"He saw nothing to exchange, only what he could take to keep and to own," the ceasg continued, barely caring for the attention of her audience. "Let his fool's tongue rot, for only I rule this sea!"

Fiadh saw an opening, a chance for more information that she had not imagined she might find out here upon the water, of a name that Eònan and Brianan had spoken to her, that of the true architect of the fall of Tur Eumor. "What of the Red Raven?" she shouted up. "I have heard it is she who truly rules these waves."

The wind seemed to quiet to a whisper as the ceasg's eyes dimmed, cast directly towards Fiadh's own as her sinuous body leaned down towards her, those pearled teeth fixing into a snarl, her muscles bunching about her neck and down to the violent veins bulging from taloned hands.

Fiadh steadied herself, fixing her expression in one of desperate determination, digging her nails into her palms to steady the shakes which threatened to seize her as she felt the ceasg's pungent breath all along her body.

Then the ceasg recoiled, her sudden movement shifting the entire ship beneath Fiadh's feet, and her laughter keened into the moonlit sky.

"Oh, you are clever little bird," her voice sprung back as she loomed, her shadow once more framed by the moon above. "To taunt me so. But you are not clever enough. I have a deal with the Raven, and you will not beckon rage from my lips by dangling her name before me." She paused, as if weighing the life held before her against something Fiadh could not yet see. "Still, I have owed the Ríagan a favour for a long while, and perhaps it is this day I might settle my debt."

"Ask me your questions, child of the Sciathán Dubh," she said. "And let me pay my final debt to your departed gods with words, to match her own favour to me."

"Where is she?" The words escaped Fiadh's lips as though they had been waiting for this moment all along. Her heart sank as the words were answered by a bark of laughter.

"This merry circle of gifts and favours between us spins like a whirlpool, child, that may one day drag us all down into the depths," she said, a cruel grin etched into her features. "I cannot answer this question, for that is the one gift I granted the Raven, that no one could possibly discover the path to her keep without magic greater than I can wield. You may find it, one day, from a being capable of granting you that very wish. But it will not be by my hand."

"Who will it be from?" Fiadh said, the words coming in a rush now, her mind whirling and stabbing at the vast nothing she knew of the Raven, nothing but the ravings of a man haunted by ghosts and the dark prophesies of a druid who refused to grant her more. It grew greater now understanding all the knowledge held by this creature of the seas.

"A creature of gold and wishes, that dances upon the graves of the dead and the light of the sun. A creature trapped as I am on this side of the glimmering arc."

"What is the arc?" Fiadh asked, her hand subconsciously reaching for the sack at her hip where the fabric she had taken from the Order resided. She remembered the passages she had opened with it, the way shadows had poured from behind it beneath the temple in the Three Willows.

"The arc is what guards your world from Fearann Eeile, the lands the gods of old reside in. You have passed through doors to the arc to the place between, where dreams and mischief is wrought." The ceasg leaned closer, those bright eyes lighting Fiadh's face from within her leering skull. "I smell it upon you, I can taste its dark residues seeping from you like a stain. I can hear his voice, the one beyond who whispers, seeking always to tear a hole in the arc and bring his people back from beyond, from where they were rightly sealed after the great battle. The Raven knows this and knows that to permit the way to be open again would be to see her power on this earth challenged by the very gods spilling forth anew."

Fiadh shook her head. The machinations of gods and monsters were beyond her. They would not get her closer to her goal, or that of Caerdrich, to avenge the fall of the Tur. There had to be something here that would bring her closer, that could be pulled from the ceasg's tales.

"You saw me fall from Tur Eumor, great one," she said, restraining a wince as she met the bright eyes that loomed over her. "Who else was there alongside the ships of the Raven and those of Ghav Rhien? There were three, I know, but one remains lost to me."

"Remember the banners that flew over the Tur when you fell from the rocks, little bird," came her answer. "They struck a bargain by summoning the Raven once and they could do so once again."

Fiadh thought back, tried to remember the glimpses of battle at the Tur, the ships that had arrived on the shore and warriors who had poured forth to begin their ascent to the ancient fortress of the Sciathán Dubh. She remembered the sails bearing the sigil of the Red Raven. She saw the shields bearing the crest of Eònan of Ghav Rhien. She saw the banners sewn with a ship and a lightning bolt.

A banner she had not seen since the fall. How had she not remembered it before? How had she not searched for it long ago?

What spells did the ceasg weave that brought it to her now, and could they be trusted? Were they truly her own memories, or creations this being planted to shape its own designs on the realms of the sea? Were they planted to lead Fiadh to her own goals, or to take her away from the horn and out again to her death willingly, without the protection it might grant her?

The ceasg smiled, "your thoughts reveal too much, small one. I may not hear the words but I can feel the storm, the yearning, the pull of power to seek something more. It is not simply the ring for which you have come into my domain."

"Nothing more, I am not here for her, nor am I here for the sea." Fiadh steadied her eyes as best she could, willing her thoughts to still, to turn away from the bargain struck with the blade and its call to the horn.

The moon shone free now, its light scattering across the waves and bathing the ship in its pale glow.

"You lie to me, little bird, you know the price paid for such deception, and yet still, you lie." The ceasg's words lapped at her thoughts, gently pulling at her to step back towards the waters.

The ceasg's words swimming in her mind were not sounds alone. They could feel her thoughts as well, they stroked the truths she had not given, coaxing them forth.

"I… seek the horn, as well, yes." The words leapt free of their own accord.

The ceasg smiled, the smile of a predator that has ensnared their prey. "Now, prove to me your worth, little one," she said. "The man you sought could not look me in the eye and tell me the truth, for he could not accept the truth within him, that his desire was selfish, not noble. That he was little better than a slaver, bent on possessing a woman regardless of her will."

"Show me you deserve the waves more than he, servant of the Ríagan, warrior of the vainglorious Sciathán Dubh! They call you Crow, upon the land, do they not? How far you have fallen from the songs of your masters. Tell me your truth. You seek the horn, no? But for what purpose, selfish or noble?"

"I seek it for revenge," she said, lifting her face to look straight into the ceasg's eyes, as dark as the water's depths, each carrying a spark of the moon's light.

"Your own, or for another?" the ceasg asked. "You are not alone in this journey and, though I need not ask, my curiosity compels me. The sea will know, and may it take you should you fail. Even Caerdrich could not free you should the sea find you wanting, for it was not the blade that lifted you up from the frozen waters below Tur Eumor."

"The blade and I have a deal, yes," Fiadh replied. "Their revenge and my own is intertwined. The justice we seek will be found together?"

"But of course," the ceasg hissed. "It is truth you speak, but there is more truth to it than even you know. You walk so far, young one, yet you see so little."

Its words were meaningless, no more than kindling to the flame of its fascination with tales and song. Fiadh had what she had come for, and more besides. She would be leaving with her life, proof of the brother's death, and information that could lead her to the Raven at last. Now only the return remained. "Will the merrow grant me passage?" she asked, daring to turn her head to see if she could spy the lantern upon the shore.

"Oh, no, little bird." The ceasg's words swam in her mind once more with undisguised mirth. "Who am I to deny them their prey? No, you must find your way home through their waters without my interference. Should you fall into the deep, then it will be clear you have not earned your return to shore, and the sea will keep you both."

Fiadh shivered, almost able to feel the damp touch of the sea creatures grasping and dragging her towards the sea floor. The ceasg spoke of fate and portents, but she knew the sea was a fickle thing that cared little for such trifling concerns as the visions of the Ríagan and the weave of the Norns.

"A deal!" she shouted. "I can bring you what was once yours, return her to the sea, and in exchange I shall take the horn so that I might call on the waves in my own time of need."

The ceasg chuckled, its heaving form sending tremors through the wood at Fiadh's feet.

"Clever bird!" came its voice. "All this time threading through your true purpose and finally you seize what might bring you what you truly want." The Ceasg stretched and Fiadh felt it, the fading of Caerdrich's icy grip, a blade satisfied.

"A pact it shall be, Crow, you may depart my ship with what you seek. But should you walk the land again, and reconsider whether to keep your side of our bargain..."

The ceasg smiled, those shimmering teeth shining like precious stones in the moonlight. "You may have the horn, wield its call to the waves, but the waves are but a part of the sea. I can wait a hundred years for you to face your fate if you do not return what is owed to me."

"Can you spend the rest of your days living in fear of every loch, every storm, every tide? You know better, I think, Crow. Do not dawdle, I will await her return with eagerness."

The ceasg drew back, the moon's light sparkling across wet scales and teeth alike.

"Fly, little bird, and should you part with the horn without bringing the sea its due, I will come for you, one day. The sea always claims what it is owed."

Those final words slithered from the creature's lips as she slipped behind the bow, scales sliding over the wooden flesh of that proud figurehead pointing to the sky, and silently into the lapping water beyond.

Fiadh stood alone once more, her feet set wide upon that slanted and shattered deck, alone with that great engraved horn held in eagles' talons. It must have rested there for years, decades, centuries even without being swept out to sea. Through the darkest storms and the greatest tides, it had sat waiting on this deck, whether waiting alone or dragged from the grip of those who had sought to make it their own.

This is what the brother had come for, and now she would hold it, a tool for seizing the waters that had borne those dark ships across the waters to the feet of Tur Eumor. A power not even the Raven could wield, an advantage, after waiting so long in the shadows and scrounging through the dirt left in her wake.

The ceasg had warned her the sea would judge her, but she knew the sea well. She knew it was vengeful and vindictive, capable of snatching away lives at a moment to claim what it wished or to repay a slight against its name. It could swallow up towns and peoples along its edge just as easily as it had provided for them, it would bear people on great voyages of adventure and discovery only to dash them against the rocks before they could return to share their tales.

She knew the sea, and the sea knew her. It understood vengeance, and it would understand her call to be true, driven by that singular cause alone. She would not call it without cause, and she would return what it was due when her time had come. Just as she had pledged to return its due should she return to place her feet upon the land.

It would not find her wanting, and if it deemed that insufficient, she now held the means to bear her beyond its reach.

Fiadh reached forward and pushed her hand through the shimmering air around the horn. The magics dimmed as her hand neared it and faded to nothing as her fingers touched the engraved metal that wrapped its form. It would not return till the call to the sea echoed from it.

Caerdrich lay silent, the cold gone from the air around her. The blade recognised power and respected it, even if they sometimes did not respect Fiadh's own. Perhaps, however, they had crossed paths with this horn in an era before her time, out upon this wide sea where emerald ships had once carved the waves. One day she might hear those tales, when the sword's thirst was finally sated.

She sequestered the horn away in the sack she hung beneath her cloak and spared only a parting glance at that shattered figurehead still reaching out towards the moon before jumping over the edge of the ship and making her way back down the wreck she had clambered up to reach here.

The rowboat still sat half-beached upon the rock. When she neared it, Fiadh saw what she had sought here in the first place. A small iron ring sat upon its lone seat, still ringed with seawater as if swept to its rest by a chance wave dashing against the rock. She took it, ran it through her hands, and stashed it away beside the horn.

Time, finally, to depart this frightful and ancient place. With a shove, she, the horn, and the blade were back out over the sea, her oars returning to the water to begin distancing them from that green-wreathed ship.

A glance over her shoulder away from the moon's light revealed her destination, the faint golden light shimmering in the distance, far from the shadow of the cliffs.

Annis still held the lantern high, at least.

The stillness of the water brought by the storm's passing brought her some respite, a chance to catch her breath and collect her thoughts. Her strokes with the oars helped steady her breathing, the pounding of her heart easing to a gentle rhythm.

Yet it was in that quiet within that she could hear the keening from the cliffs, worming its way through the wax, caressing her skull, setting hairs on end. The merrow knew she had returned to the water.

She spared another glance towards the shore, seeing the mists that carried their wails clouding the surface, obscuring the way, leaving only the faintest golden glow of the lantern on the beach.

They were circling her once more, the mists pressing closer, the water slapping against the sides of her craft even though the water beyond sat still. Fins and scales began to break the surface, dipping in and out of view as the keening grew to a tumult, demanding she listen, to tear out the wax and give in to the cries.

She could feel the claws pawing at her leathers, one drawing up and brushing at her hair, drifting along her cheek. She shuddered at its touch but gritted her teeth against the fear, refusing to give them her gaze or let them distract her. To let them have her attention for even a moment would be enough for them to drag her down into the cold with them.

Fiadh closed her eyes, steadied her breathing, and focussed on the rhythm of the oars. She set her mind on the feeling of lifting them from the water, reaching forward, touching them down, and pulling back, on the tension running through her forearms as she drummed her fingers on the wood to ease the tension of her grip. She flexed out the renewed burning sensation, running from her shoulders to the hollow of her back, rolling free of it as she brought the oars back, tensing against the pressure as she pulled back.

One stroke at a time, pushing through the mist, her ears dead to the sound beyond her wooden vessel. Toward the light still shrouded in mist.

Then she jolted forwards, the rowboat coming to an abrupt halt as it slammed up against the pebbles, the crunch of wood on stone sending vibrations shuddering up her bones.

Snatching up her sack, patting it to check the ring and horn were still safely within, Fiadh leapt over the side and scampered up the beach, putting as much distance as she could between herself and the water. She tore the wax free, immediately hearing the roar of water and wind, and of her feet sliding about on the rocks. Finally, the pebbles were lit by the golden glow of the lantern, which stood alone, propped up on the top of a long branch of driftwood.

Annis himself sat halfway up the beach, perched on the pebbles, one hand holding a lump of wood and the other a dirk, surrounded by chipped splinters and slivers he'd loosened.

"Whit?" came his complaint as she stomped up the pebbles towards him. "Ah wisnae gonnae juist staun ther till mah airm gave oot," he gave a shrug.

"Besides, ah wanted tae ken if ah cuid mak' a fish oot o' this 'ere wood." He waved it in her direction and pushed himself to his feet. "Turns oot ah cannae. Ah'm no sure how onybody wid mak yin. It looks a richt mess."

"I could have died!" her own voice caught her by surprise, sounding more as a dry croak than the authoritative tone she had intended. "If there'd been no light to cast the way, I could have been led anywhere, you'd have been waiting here till my corpse washed ashore!"

As she strode up to him Annis stood, and Fiadh was more disgruntled than ever to be confronted by his chest, having to crane her neck to look him in the eyes.

Another shrug, and Annis waved in the direction of the torch. "Ah kin see it, ah held it fast. Ah kept an eye oan it, niver fret, ah'd huv kept it staunin' till the sun came up an' drooned oot the licht."

Annis looked at her, his nose slightly crinkled.

"What?" she coughed, feeling the sting of salt scalding her throat.

"Whin the moon's oot at nicht yer eyes licht up, even

whin yer facing awa' fae it. Ah ken the eyes o' cats or deer micht shine wi' the light o' a torch. Bit yers shine thair ain licht. It's nae richt, it gives me the wullies. Ah dinnae like it."

She knew how he felt, for once, looking back over the waters towards the rock framed in the moon's light. Fiadh had no doubt that if she and the ceasg ever crossed paths again, it would be when the sea had called for her to be returned to it, permanently. Those star-bright eyes would follow her, a memory to haunt sleepless nights as a reminder that far greater powers rested in the corners of this earth than her and the blade she bore.

But not on land, for now, at least.

"Aye, Annis, it's not right, but you're going to have to deal with it for a while longer at least. For now, we have a merchant to visit," she said, beginning her crunching steps up the pebbled beach.

"A merchant?"

"Yeah, one who took something from the sea that wasn't his to take. It's about time he returned it."

***

Fiadh sat on her heels behind the dock's wall, peering around a barrel left at its base towards the merchant's sprawling home. The road before it was cobbled rather than mud, still slick with the rain and sea spray from earlier in the night.

A low wall sat around its base, two floors of fine log-hewn structure rising beyond them in a trio of buildings boarded by shutters embellished with the merchant's personal sigil, a clear challenge to the power of the Rìgh.

Annis stood languidly behind her, leaning back against the dock.

"How mony?" he grumbled, rubbing the tiredness from his eyes.

"Just one," she whispered in reply. "But one's plenty if all they need do is raise a shout and anyone with coin in his master's ventures comes running with axe and pitchfork."

The guard was practically asleep at his station, his hardened leather helm from beneath his hood reflecting the blues and hints of gold from the encroaching dawn. His head was slumped, but he'd clearly found a nook in the loose stonework that prevented him toppling in his half-slumber.

"So, how do we do this?" she said back to her companion, who looked moments away from drifting off himself.

"One guard at the door," she continued. "Might be a chance to get in around the back? These kinds of places always have another entrance…"

"Nah, dinnae worry, it'll be quiet," Annis said, brushing past her shoulder and barely pausing in his stride as he walked directly across the paving and up to the entrance.

The guard jumped for a moment, hand gripped fast about his spear, and looked ready to challenge the intruder when Annis' palm fixed over his face and slammed his head into the wall behind him.

He crumpled to the ground, silent.

Fiadh jogged up beside him. "Is… is he dead?" she said as he nudged the prone body with a foot.

Annis shrugged. "Mebbe, Ah'm no sure. Ah'll put money oan his bein' back oan his feet shortly, wi' a poundin' heid an' a sense o' impendin' unemployment."

"We don't kill here, Annis, that's not what we're here for. We don't need to drive these people into the hands of the Order" she said, her voice still subconsciously a whisper.

Annis turned his head with eyebrows knotted in scepticism, "then mebbe ye ought tae huv mentioned it so ah'd ken it afore noo, Craw."

Fiadh shook her head and gave the path on either side of them a final look for any incoming trouble before moving through the open gateway and up to the door of the merchant's property.

The door itself was a simple affair, not locked by key as many of the properties of the wealthy to the south had come to be of late. Fiadh ran her hands over her knives, stopping at one with a long blade and handle, long blunted by its use as a tool and more suitable for this kind of task than as a weapon.

She slid it gently along the gap between the door and its mounting, feeling it drift and then bump over the bar that held it in place. Crouching, she took another blade and pinned it lengthwise along the door and into the frame.

Then, at Fiadh's signal, Annis stepped forward and rammed both hands down on the first blade's handle hard. Barely a moment of resistance followed as it pivoted, and they heard a clatter from within.

Fiadh pulled her blade free and beckoned Annis forward, following behind as he swung the door loose and they entered the room beyond.

Their welcome came swiftly.

"Who are you?"

The merchant stood framed in the candlelight of the

stairs, dressed only in a tunic that barely covered his particulars. The veins of his neck protruded beneath beetroot jowls and eyes bulging with rage. Salted whiskers completed the comic display.

The room was far more spacious than the carpenter's. A fire pit sat embedded in a stone-framed wall, a table with seating for a dozen men filled its centre, and smooth-hewn wooden beams held up a ceiling which could well support more rooms above. The hearth holding the smouldering coals was embellished with trophies and gifts that must have come from far across the seas, bearing runes and scripts that were alien and ornate.

Above them all, framed high above the fire, was a folded fur as long as a man, pinned in place by wooden pegs hammered deep into the stonework.

"We're here for your captive, you are free to stand aside," Fiadh responded, gesturing Annis towards the hanging sealskin.

"I will not!" came his growled reply as he stomped down the steps. He must have been a larger man in his day, maybe once inches taller than Annis and broader still, though his bulk had long since slid from his muscles into signs of a far more comfortable existence.

"Annis, if you would," Fiadh said.

He looked between her and the merchant at her bemused, having barely moved from the door.

"The skin over the hearth please, it's what we're here for and you're taller than me."

He frowned, nodded, and moved in its direction. The merchant stammered for a moment and then moved as if to block his path.

Annis jabbed a finger in his direction. "You'll haud

yersel there, wee man," he growled. "Or else Ah'll be puttin' yer heid through these here coals."

The merchant came to an abrupt halt. Fiadh could not have told whether he spoke Ardish, there was every chance he didn't, but the message seemed clear enough regardless.

"Wee man?" she whispered to Annis as she accompanied him towards the hearth, keeping her eyes on the man who seemed trapped between simmering rage and fear as Annis' hands approached the hearth.

Annis shoved a stool over towards the hearth and clambered upon it. "Aye," he said. "Wee is a state o' mind, no a stature, an' this yin here is full tae the brim wi' it."

Fiadh stopped moving as she saw motion behind the merchant. He was not alone at the stairs. Crouched behind him, one hand around the wooden pillar and at arm's reach from the man, crouched a figure clad only in a light shift. Her long limbs spread in a stance somewhere between a coiled predator and prey preparing to flee.

It seemed they had the attention of the one they had come for.

Annis grunted as he hauled himself up closer to the hide and began to tug at the wooden stakes that held it in place. "Careful," Fiadh hissed. "Bring it down in one piece. It's worth more than we can pay to return it undamaged."

The merchant stammered again and began to stomp across the room. Fiadh spotted what he was moving towards, a hatchet set upon the wall. She moved swiftly, a hand running to the blades strapped along her torso, pulling one free and pointing it towards the man.

"Hold yourself there," she spat in Cànan. He barely spared her a glance, not so much as slowing his steps as he clasped both hands around the axe's long haft and pulled it free, snarling.

He turned towards her and they stood there in silence for a moment, his furious glare meeting her steady one, her blade held out towards him and his across his chest.

He was slower now than he may have been when he had last wielded a weapon, but he held it with the certainty of a man who had once carved his own way through the world.

Fiadh had used her blades when needed over the years, but she was no fighter. Annis was paid for that particular role, and more often enough his size was imposing enough to discourage it. If it came to blows, she was not sure she could avoid that curved blade, and from the size of it she couldn't be certain a single blow would not be enough.

"Ah huv it!" Annis words split the air between them, and she spared a glance at him as he proudly held the hide over his head, unfolding it into long brown sealskin as he stretched it out almost as wide as his arms could hold it.

"Great, now, put it down, Annis," she said, keeping her blade hand steady towards the merchant.

"Whit? Ah thocht we needed it."

"We don't." Fiadh jerked her head towards the stairs. "She does."

The figure in the stairs had made her way to them in almost complete silence as she moved gently on the bare balls of her feet. Her eyes were fixed on Annis, flitting between his face and the skin he held overhead.

"Ah dinnae think she needs a…"

"Don't think," Fiadh snapped. "Put it down."

He looked uncertain as he gently lowered his arms down, all three of them flitting their eyes back and forth between the others in the room.

But as he began to set the sealskin down at his feet, the merchant broke the silence with a bellowing "NO!" and made to barge past Fiadh towards Annis.

But another among them was faster still. As soon as the skin touched the floor, the silent figure lunged across between them and, before Fiadh could so much as turn towards her, had seized hold of Fiadh's hand and twisted the knife free from her grasp.

The sudden twisted grip had Fiadh stumbling to the side, free from the swing of the merchant's axe which came down between them. It was the only swing he would be given.

The knife spun from one hand to the other and slashed across the man's bare arms, crisscrossing them, streaks of crimson flying across the walls and floor. The merchant released the hatchet and stumbled back as the slices continued to cut ribbons from his arms, raised to shield his face.

The knife fell, and, taken up by the selkie's other hand, it plunged into the man's thigh and twisted, pulling a cry of pain free from him as he fell to one knee and then fell prone to the floor. The selkie continued to press towards him, her foot planted on his chest, shoving him to the ground. The blade screeched as it met stone in the ground beneath him, the sound weaving with his screams.

Fiadh's heels kicked at the ground as she tried to shift herself clear of the grappling pair, she felt Annis' hands grip her under her arms and haul her back and clear as the sickening sound of the blade scratching the flagstones set her teeth on edge. She cringed, torn between fixation on the animalistic display of rage and turning her head away from it as the selkie's hands rose up and plunged down, beating the merchant's head against the ground.

Then the girl straddled him, pinning his arms to his sides between her thighs as he attempted to writhe free, screaming as every movement tore the blade in his leg further through his flesh.

The selkie snarled, her hands fixed over his face. Her muscles bunched as her thumbs pressed down on his eyelids, palms clamped firmly against his cheeks to hold his head in place. She kept pushing even as his screams rose into a shriek, blood seeping out of his sockets before, with a sickening pop, her thumbs plunged into his skull and his entire body spasmed and fell still.

"Fuck," Annis whispered in shock. The pair of them had stayed frozen between the doorway and the hearth, Fiadh still sprawled against the wall at his feet, neither able to tear their eyes free even as the selkie rose from the merchant's still body, crimson droplets falling from her hands.

"He will never covet another with that twisted gaze again," she spat as she stood over the merchant's unmoving form, the words dancing in the musical Cànan the ceasg had spoken directly into Fiadh's mind. "He'll travel to Tech Duinn blind and wander there forevermore, never able to find the way on to rest."

"Fuck," came Annis' reply, still frozen at the hearth and none the wiser for the words spoken in a language he did not share.

The selkie moved towards him and he broke his

stillness to back away from the hearth, the skin still laid at its mouth. She knelt before it and lifted it gently, one hand trailing across the fur with care and longing, her fingertips smoothing the hairs even as they seemed to follow her touch.

Where once the hide had been inanimate, the skin a faded leather as if tanned to be stitched, it now sprung to life, warm and soft, the skin moving along with the selkie's fingertips as if it were to rise up and wreath them with its warmth.

She stood, the living skin held across her blood-stained hands, and turned towards Fiadh still breathing heavily upon the floor.

"You did not come to lay claim to what is mine, girl?" she asked, paying no heed to Annis though he stood close by and with a hand upon the hilt of his blade.

"No," Fiadh shook her head, rolling back to her feet and dusting off her clothes. "I have come on behalf of the sea so that you may return to it."

"For what?" The selkie's tone was harsh, suspicious, even as the words danced from her lips.

"The deal has been struck already and I have what I sought from the waves," Fiadh said, meeting her gaze, searching the eyes that swam with blues and greens. "I have nothing more to claim, only that I may ease your path back to the water."

The selkie's gaze was still, unreadable, and with no further words, she turned and made her way to the door and out into the soft golden light of the rising dawn.

Fiadh leant and pulled her knife free from the still leg of the merchant, trying not to meet his eyeless visage but unable to escape its slack, empty gaze. There was something less scarring to it than the faded eyes of the dead she had seen before, but the violence of his end would stick with her, she knew, as a reminder of what the sea could bring to the shore.

As she turned and moved through the door, she heard Annis behind her, turned to see him cradling the merchant's axe with some mix of guilt and joy in his smile.

"Stealing from the dead, now, is it?" she said, more amused than anything else.

"Aye, weel, it's no lik' he'll be needing it, an' given how it did him nae guid I've nae doubt his spirit wid want it taken far awa'. No reason fur me nae tae dae him the favour."

Fiadh shrugged. If the gods wanted to punish him for it, she was sure they'd find a way. Maybe at least this way he'd have a weapon to fend off whatever curse they sent to them. She had plenty lined up for them both already.

The selkie stood still where the pebbles of the shore met the land, the shore grasses and her shift waving with the breeze, her head held high as she looked out over the waters, skin in hand.

Fiadh walked up beside her, hearing Annis come to a stop on the path where he no doubt intended to hold watch whilst staying far from the reach of those blood-stained hands.

"You have the horn, then?" the selkie asked, not taking her eyes off the warming horizon.

Fiadh nodded, enjoying the sound of the lapping waters for a time. "I do," she said, eventually.

"What will you do with it?" she asked, turning to look at her.

"I have a promise to keep that I hope, with its help,

I might finally bring to rest. It's been too long, and I've travelled too far, to let it wait any longer," Fiadh replied.

The sun was beginning to break over the horizon, causing Fiadh to wince against the glare shining off the waters.

"What of the man who went searching for the horn before I came here?" she asked the selkie in return. "His brother said he came here for you, waited for you at the dockside."

The selkie responded with confusion for a moment and then with a snarl filled with contempt.

"I remember him." Her tone dripped with derision. "We never exchanged so much as a word, but I felt his eyes on me. I know that look, that impotent greed so much more intense than desire alone. He did not search for love, he sought to possess something that was not his own. That is how he saw me, as a thing, no different to how the merchant did."

She removed a hand from beneath the seal pelt, raising it so Fiadh could see the dark mark that ran across her forearm, beyond where the blood halted. She could see the shape of a hand, fingers wrapped about it, like it had been burned into her skin.

"It was not the merchant who marked me so, but the sailor," she spat. "He grew the courage to grab me, once, tried to drag me away. I was wailing my pain, feeling my skin being pulled away from me still pinned to the merchant's wall, but he kept pulling at me even as I warned him I could go no further. He only let me go when he saw the mark begin to spread and knew what he desired would be too marred by the loss of my skin for him to enjoy, should he have dragged me further."

The look in the selkie's eyes was merciless, cold, what

they had seen for a flash as she'd lunged across the merchant's hall and taken Fiadh's blade from her.

"Is he dead?" the selkie asked, her gaze fixed on Fiadh now. She nodded her reply.

"They were no different, he and the merchant," she continued. "No amount of wealth could divide the cruelty both held within them. Both would have claimed my skin, never to return it had the sea not intervened."

"So no, I do not feel regret for his passing," she said, answering the question Fiadh had not thought to ask. "He wished to claim power over the sea to sate his greed, and in turn, the sea took him as its own. A fitting fate."

Fiadh reached into her sack and rummaged for the small piece of metal she was searching for, she pulled it out and turned the ring over in her palm, letting the iron glint in the dawn's light and touch upon the two fish intertwined on its surface. So simple a gift, given with so much heart, and given away with so little.

A crunch of shifting pebbles alerted her that the selkie wasn't looking along with her. She had begun her descent towards the water, the furs in her arms beginning to shift and run from her hands over her arms, gradually enveloping her skin as the shift fell away.

Fiadh watched as the fur encased her like a shell, pulling her arms and legs close, her feet forming flippers and whiskers springing from the brown cheeks.

As smooth as she had walked from the hall, the seal slid into the waters and vanished from view, barely leaving so much as a ripple on the surface behind it.

Fiadh turned the ring over in her hand once more and turned back towards the merchant's hall, seeing Annis had watched the selkie's departure as well. They exchanged a nod as she approached, and Fiadh looked back over the water once more, seeking that lonely rock in the distance, framed by the rising sun.

Annis coughed, and when he next spoke it was in a baritone verse.

"Ah yince knew a lass,
who cam fae the sea,
bourne by the waves,
carried hame tae me.

But ye dinnae haud a lass,
by leash or by gold,
else they'll sprout wings an' fly,
and lea yer hearth cauld."

They stood in silence a while longer, looking out over the waters as the glimmer of sunlight lit the crests of the waves as they swept over the pebbled bay.

"Ma faithir taucht me that yin, a lang time ago," he said to the silence. "Ma mither left afore ah kent her, but ah aye thocht she likely bolted frae him. Ye cuid see it in his eyes, ye ken, that yearning fur something he knew he lost through nae fault but his ain."

Fiadh wasn't quite sure how to respond to that. She'd had no parents of her own, nor had she allowed herself to come to know any of the families who had given her refuge in the years following her fall from Tur Eumor. The concept of staying alongside anyone for years, decades even? She'd seen too many gone before their time to have any faith that they could ever stay. There had been many before Annis, no doubt there would be many more after him.

"Would you have gone to sea for a lass like that, Annis?" she asked, tilting her head towards the shore.

He shrugged, shaking his head. "No, she wasnae my kind. I prefer those wi a wee bit more… heft, if ye ken whit I mean."

Fiadh shrugged in turn. She didn't, truly. These people's urges for one another, enough to turn to such cruelty or even throw away their lives for, was as alien to her as a life of a selkie beneath the waves.

"But ye ken, that lass cuid mair than hauf handle herself, mebbe she'll fin herself someone afore lang."

"... afore lang?" Fiadh pinched her nose as she tried to understand Annis' unique phrasing. "She'll be older than the oldest house in this entire town, Annis."

"Aye well ye cannae just write an older lass aff lik' that, onybody hus it in thaim tae change."

Fiadh snorted and turned away from the water, giving the ring a final look before handing it to Annis.

"See that the brother gets this, Annis, and that we get our due," she said, tipping the iron band into his hand. "Tell him that he's perished, dragged beneath the waves by the merrow, and that I fell to the same fate. That you were the only one of us to get to shore."

She raised her hood, aware that, with the growing light of the dawn, it was only so long before people began to emerge from their homes around Tur Pailt.

"Yer deid noo?" he mumbled, looking over the ring himself.

"As far as this town is concerned, yes. I died at sea. I'm sure it's not an expected way for a Crow to go, dragged down by the very monsters they hire us to rid them of. You heard him, yesterday, the Order has been looking for us already, and maybe they could use a disincentive to continue their search."

"So, I'll catch up wi` ye at the horses. Whaur next, Craw?"

"Next we look for a ship's banner with a lightning bolt over the waves. There's another who believes us Crows long dead who I believe needs to discover that he left one behind."

ABOUT THE AUTHOR

Tristan Gray was a latecomer to Scotland, moving to the north from Jersey in 2014.

After years of searching to find the real spark behind his writing Scotland unlocked it - The rugged country and dark history, which also inspired the works of George R. Martin and Diana Gabaldon, gave new meaning to the fantasy tales of his childhood.

Now, with a new connection to an adopted home driving his work, and inspiration stretching from conventional novels, to graphic novels, to games, Tristan is writing tales worthy of the inspiration by the land around him.

He can be found at his website:
tristangraywrites.com

Milton Keynes UK
Ingram Content Group UK Ltd.
UKHW020812150823
426904UK00018B/857

9 781838 485443